For Flora and Kit, in memory of
their great-grandmother — M. F.

For Alfie, Faith, Joe and Max,
with love — K. S.

The little Red Hen

Written by Mary Finch
Illustrated by Kate Slater
Narrated by Debra Messing

Barefoot Books
step inside a story

Once upon a time, a rooster and a mouse
and a little red hen lived together in a
small brown house with a red roof.

One day, the little red hen found a grain of wheat lying on the ground. "Look what I've found," she said to the rooster and the mouse.

"I will plant it in the earth. Who will help me?"

"Not I," said the rooster.
"Not I," said the mouse.
"Then I'll do it myself," said the little red hen.

She scratched at the earth and **planted** the grain.

"Who will help me water it?"
asked the little red hen.

"Not I," said the rooster.
"Not I," said the mouse.
"Then I'll do it myself,"
said the little red hen.

She **watered** the earth and **waited** for the wheat to grow. The sun shone, and the wheat grew tall and straight. When the ear of wheat was golden, she asked:

"Who will help me harvest it?"

"Not I," said the rooster.
"Not I," said the mouse.
"Then I'll do it myself," said the little red hen.

She **picked** the ear of wheat and put it in a basket. "Who will help me take it to the mill to be ground into flour?" asked the little red hen.

"Not I," said the rooster.
"Not I," said the mouse.
"Then I'll do it myself," said the little red hen.

The miller **ground** the ear of wheat into fine white flour.

"Who will help me make this flour into dough?" asked the little red hen.

"Not I," said the rooster.
"Not I," said the mouse.
"Then I'll do it myself,"
said the little red hen.

She **mixed** the flour into warm, yeasty dough.

"Who will help me knead this dough into bread?" asked the little red hen.

"Not I," said the rooster.
"Not I," said the mouse.
"Then I'll do it myself," said the little red hen.

She **kneaded** the dough again, left it
to rise, then **shaped** it into a round, shiny loaf.

"Who will help me put this loaf into the oven?"
asked the little red hen.

"Not I," said the rooster.
"Not I," said the mouse.
"Then I'll do it myself,"
said the little red hen.

She **put** the loaf into the oven to bake.
When it was ready, she **took out** the
warm, crusty loaf.

"Who will help me eat this tasty, fresh bread?"
asked the little red hen.

"I will," said the rooster.
"I will," said the mouse.

"No you won't," said the little red hen.
"I shall eat it myself," said the little red hen.

And she did!

"Oh," said the rooster

So the next time the little red hen **found** a grain of wheat lying on the ground...
the rooster **scratched** at the earth and **planted** the grain,

the mouse **watered** the earth,

And together, the rooster and the mouse and the little
red hen **watched** the wheat grow tall and straight.

Together they **took** the wheat to the miller to **grind** it into flour, and together they **mixed** the flour to make the dough.

And when the bread was ready, the rooster and the mouse and the little red hen sat down together and **ate** the nice, warm loaf...

and it was delicious!

Bake your own tasty bread!

Makes: 2 loaves (or lots of small bread rolls)

Things you will need

- A big bowl
- A cloth to cover the bowl
- A baking sheet or two small loaf pans
- Olive or vegetable oil
- A helpful adult

Ingredients for the bread

- 750g or 7½ c whole grain or whole meal bread flour
- 400ml or 1½ c warm water
- 2 tsp dried yeast
- 1 tsp flaky or small sea salt

How to make your bread

1 Stirring

Put the flour, yeast and salt into a bowl. Make a hole in the pile of ingredients. Pour the warm water (this should be body temperature) into the hole bit by bit, and stir the mixture with your fingers, until you have used up all the water and have a slightly tacky dough.

Ask an adult to boil the water for you. You need 1 part hot boiled water to 3 parts cold water.

2 Kneading

Knead the ball of dough just like the little red hen does. On a lightly-floured surface, knead the dough by pulling the dough outwards and then pressing it back into the middle of the ball with your knuckles. Keep doing this until the dough looks smooth. This should take about five minutes. You can add a little more flour to stop the dough being too sticky. When the dough is smooth, keep kneading it for another five minutes.

Don't be gentle — put a lot of effort in! It's important to get lots of air in the mixture to help the yeast make the dough rise.

3 Proving

Shape the kneaded dough into a good firm ball again. Place it back in the bowl and ask an adult to cut a cross in the top with a sharp knife. This will let the dough rise, or "**prove**". Cover the bowl with a damp cloth and leave it in a nice warm place to rise for about an hour and a half. The dough is ready when it has doubled in size.

Make the loaves any shape you want

4 Shaping

Lightly grease the baking sheet/loaf pan. When the dough has risen, place it on the sheet/pan and shape it into loaves. When you have shaped your bread, turn on the oven for 15 minutes to heat up to 200⁰ C or 400° F. While the oven heats up, the dough will rise again — this is called the "second prove".

5 Baking

When your oven is hot enough, and the dough has risen again, bake the loaves for around 30 minutes (20–25 minutes for rolls). When they are golden brown and look yummy, the loaves should be done. Lift them carefully up out of the tins and tap them on the bottom. If the bread sounds hollow then it is ready.

6 Eating

Leave your baked bread on a wire tray until it is cool enough to eat, and then enjoy! You could try it with butter and jam, eat it with soup or make some sandwiches. Mmmmm — delicious!

Barefoot Books
294 Banbury Road
Oxford, OX2 7ED

Barefoot Books
2067 Massachusetts Ave
Cambridge, MA 02140

First published in 2009 in Great Britain by Barefoot Books, Ltd
and in the United States of America by Barefoot Books, Inc
as *The Little Red Hen and the Ear of Wheat*
The hardback edition with CD first published in 2013
The paperback edition with CD first published in 2013
The paperback edition first published in 2013

Graphic design by Louise Millar, London
Reproduction by B & P International, Hong Kong
Printed in China on 100% acid-free paper
This book was typeset in A Font with Serifs, Garamond and Branboll
The illustrations were prepared in collage and paper-cuts
to create 3D, relief pieces which are hung from wires,
then the full compositions are photographed

Hardback with CD ISBN 978-1-84686-575-6
Paperback with CD ISBN 978-1-84686-751-4
Paperback ISBN 978-1-78285-041-0

British Cataloguing-in-Publication Data:
a catalogue record for this book is available from the British Library

Library of Congress Cataloging-in-Publication Data is available under
LCCN 2012043644

1 3 5 7 9 8 6 4 2

Barefoot Books
step inside a story

At Barefoot Books, we celebrate art and story that opens the hearts and minds of children from all walks of life, focusing on themes that encourage independence of spirit, enthusiasm for learning and respect for the world's diversity. The welfare of our children is dependent on the welfare of the planet, so we source paper from sustainably managed forests and constantly strive to reduce our environmental impact. Playful, beautiful and created to last a lifetime, our products combine the best of the present with the best of the past to educate our children as the caretakers of tomorrow.

www.barefootbooks.com

Mary Finch has always liked hens. As a child in London just after the war, her family kept hens in the garden. They had a battered and well-loved copy of this story. Mary has two daughters and two grandchildren and lives in Bath, UK.

Kate Slater lives on a dairy farm in Staffordshire, UK, with her family, her dog, lots of chickens and two pet sheep. Her studio